Disney's
Fool's Gold

ISBN: 0-7172-8434-4
Manufactured in the United States of America.   D E F   4

GROLIER
BOOK CLUB EDITION

Mickey Mouse and his friend Goofy were on a fishing trip in Alaska.

They found a nice place to camp by a mountain lake.

After setting up their camp, Mickey
and Goofy went fishing.

The fishing was really great!

Goofy chopped wood for the fire
and Mickey cleaned the fish.

The fish smelled wonderful as they
cooked over the wood fire.
    And they tasted even better!

Mickey and Goofy heard the splash
of a paddle.
  Along came an old trapper in a canoe.

"Howdy, boys," said the trapper.
"Your supper sure smells good."
So of course the boys asked
the trapper to eat with them.

After supper they sat talking around the campfire.

"Times sure have changed here," said the trapper. "In the old days everybody was looking for gold. Not everyone found it. I was one of the lucky ones."

"You mean you found gold?" cried Goofy.

"Yup," said the old trapper.

He pulled some nuggets of bright rock from his pockets.

"Lots of gold still in these mountains," he said. "Up around Twin Peaks. I could find more, but I don't need to be rich."

The next morning the trapper said good-bye
and paddled off in his canoe.

Mickey and Goofy no longer felt like fishing.

They had gold fever!

"How about paddling up to Twin Peaks?" said Mickey.

"You bet!" said Goofy.

Before nightfall they reached a town.
It was on a river near Twin Peaks.

Snow started coming down—fast!

Snow covered the ground by the time
Mickey and Goofy arrived in town.
They went right to a warm hotel.

The next day they went shopping.
They needed tools for digging gold.
And they needed snowshoes and food.

Soon Goofy
was loaded
down with
supplies.

Mickey rented a dog sled and a team of
huskies to pull it.

DOG SLEDS

Then off they went over the snowy hills.

At Twin Peaks they unloaded the sled and began to dig.

It was not easy to sink a pick or shovel into the frozen ground.

Before long Goofy turned up a nugget of bright, shiny rock.

"Hey, Mickey, look at this!" he called.
"Wow!" said Mickey. "It's gold!"

The boys worked harder and faster
than ever.

They filled two bags with shiny rocks.
Then they headed back to town.

Proudly they showed their find
to the hotelkeeper.

"Ho, ho!" laughed the hotelkeeper.
"That's not gold! It's iron pyrites.
We call it fool's gold. Don't feel bad.
These rocks have fooled plenty of people."

Mickey and Goofy were very disappointed.
But they were not ready to quit.

So the next morning they went off to
Twin Peaks once more.

This time they walked to a spot closer
to town.

While Goofy dug, Mickey looked around.
He found a cave.

Mickey crawled into the cave.
He lit a match so he could see.
Gold gleamed in the rock!

Mickey hacked
some nuggets of gold
out of the rock.

"Hey, Goofy!" he yelled. "Look at this!
This is REAL gold!"

"Wow!" said Goofy. "We're rich!"
Together they filled two bags with gold.
Then they headed back to town.

The bags of gold were very heavy.
When the boys came to Totem Pole Park,
Mickey got an idea.

"My arms are tired," said Mickey.
"Let's leave the gold inside a totem pole.
We can pick it up later with a dog sled."
    "Okay," said Goofy, and he dropped
the bags into an opening.

Mickey kept a nugget to show at the hotel.
"That's gold, all right!" said the hotelkeeper.
But he was wrong!

Two strangers heard the hotelkeeper.
They began to whisper together.

The next morning the two strangers
watched Mickey and Goofy leave the hotel.
They watched the boys get on a dog sled...

and they followed the boys to Totem Pole Park.

At first the boys did not see the other sled.

But as Mickey reached for the bags
of gold, Goofy saw the strangers coming.
"Those guys look like trouble!" said
Goofy. "Let's get out of here!"

The boys leaped onto their sled
with the gold.
Away they raced!
The strangers followed.

Up and down hill went the two dog teams.
Mickey and Goofy shouted to their dogs.
The huskies did their best.
But the strangers were better drivers.

The strangers came closer
and closer.

"They're going to catch us!"
cried Goofy.

"Throw them the gold!" yelled Mickey.
"Right," said Goofy.
The boys began to toss gold nuggets
from the sled.

The strangers stopped to pick up
the gold.
"Hey, this isn't real gold!" said
one man. "It's just fool's gold!"

Now the boys' sled was much lighter.
Mickey and Goofy raced on into town.
They returned the sled, packed up,
and paid the hotel bill.
Then they headed for the dock.

The boys got on a riverboat to start
the long journey home.

"Wow, what an adventure!" said Mickey.
"Too bad we had to give up all that gold.
But at least we're safe and sound."

"And we do have a little gold left,"
said Goofy.

He pulled out a nugget.

"I guess we weren't meant to be rich,"
said Mickey.

He didn't know how right he was—
because that nugget of gold was
fool's gold too!